FROGGY GOES TO THE DOCTOR

FROGGY GOES TO THE DOCTOR

by **JONATHAN LONDON**
illustrated by **FRANK REMKIEWICZ**

SCHOLASTIC INC.
New York Toronto London Auckland Sydney
Mexico City New Delhi Hong Kong Buenos Aires

For the good Dr. Drier & her good patient, Sean
   —J. L.

For Judi, Sue, Ruby, Harriett, Kathern, Charles, Alfred,
and Richard at the Liott Center
   —F. R.

ISBN 0-439-56226-0

Text copyright © 2002 by Jonathan London. Illustrations copyright © 2002 by Frank Remkiewicz.
All rights reserved. Published by Scholastic Inc., 557 Broadway, New York, NY 10012,
by arrangement with Viking Children's Books, a member of Penguin Group (USA) Inc.
SCHOLASTIC and associated logos are trademarks and/or registered trademarks of Scholastic Inc.

12 11 10 9 8 7 6 5 4 3 2   3 4 5 6 7 8/0

Printed in the U.S.A.   08

First Scholastic printing, September 2003

Set in Kabel

Froggy woke up.
Hurray! he thought.
No school today—
it's my check-up day!
I can get up late!

But wait! *Wait!*
What if the doctor
wants to give me a *shot*?

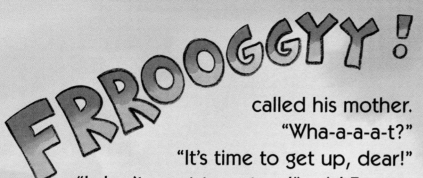

FRROOGGYY!

called his mother.
"Wha-a-a-t?"
"It's time to get up, dear!"
"I don't want to get up!" said Froggy.
"It's time for your check-up,"
said his mother. *"Now!"*

Froggy crawled out of bed
and flopped into the kitchen—
flop flop flop.

"It's time to see Dr. Mugwort,"
said his mother.
Dr. Mugwort was the wife
of Froggy's principal, Mr. Mugwort.
"I don't want to see Dr. Mugwort,"
groaned Froggy.

"I feel fine—see?"
Froggy hopped onto the table
and tried to make a muscle.
"It's just a check-up,"
said Froggy's mother.
"Now go get dressed—
and don't forget to brush
and put on clean underwear!"

So Froggy flopped back to his room
to get dressed—
flop flop flop.

At the doctor's office,
they had to sit a long time
in the waiting room.

Froggy was worried.
What if I need a shot?
Then in came Frogilina
with her mother.

"Hi, Froggy!" said Frogilina. She bounced down right beside him.

Froggy scooted away. Frogilina scooted closer.

Froggy scooted away . . .

and fell off the bench—*bonk!*

But it was hard to sit still.
He made a paper airplane
and threw it in the air—*zwish!*—
just as Dr. Mugwort stepped into the room.
It circled once . . . it circled twice . . .

then hit her smack in the eye—*zow!*
"Oops!" said Froggy.

"Follow me," said Dr. Mugwort.
She was not a happy doctor.

She told Froggy to step on the scale . . .
measured how tall he was . . .
then led him and his mother
into a room and said,
"Take off all your clothes, Froggy—
except for your underwear—
and put on this paper gown."
The doctor closed
the door behind her.

Froggy took off his shoes,
pulled off his socks,
unbuttoned his shirt,
unzipped his pants,
and looked down.

Then she cut holes in a paper pillowcase
and made a pair of underpants
held together with safety pins.
"But Mom," whined Froggy,
"they look like *diapers!*"
He quickly pulled on his
paper gown—*zeep!*

Dr. Mugwort came back in.
She took his temperature . . .
felt his tummy—
"Oh that tickles!" giggled Froggy . . .
and looked in his eyes with a light—
"Please don't cross your eyes, Froggy!"
(She didn't look in his ears—
Froggy didn't have any ears.)

Then she looked in his mouth
and said, "Say *ahhhhh*."

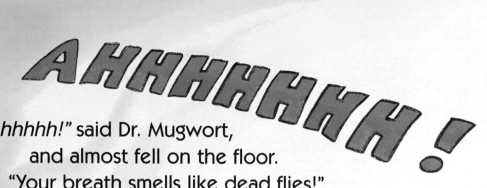

"*Ohhhhhh!*" said Dr. Mugwort,
and almost fell on the floor.
"Your breath smells like dead flies!"
"Oops!" said Froggy. "I guess I forgot to brush."

She stood up and rubbed her stethoscope.
"Now this may feel cold," she said,
and pressed it against his back.
"Yikes!" yelled Froggy.
He grabbed the stethoscope
and shouted into it,

IT'S FREEZING!

Again, Dr. Mugwort
almost fell on the floor.

Then she said, "Now Froggy, let's check your reflexes." She tapped his knee with a little rubber hammer. Nothing. She tapped it a little harder— *bonk!*—and up flew his foot right into her chin—*clack!*

This time Dr. Mugwort *did* fall on the floor.
"Oops!" cried Froggy,
looking more red in the face
than green.

Dr. Mugwort stood up
and glared at him.
"Time for your shot, Froggy," she said.

"Just kidding!"
Then she gave him a gold star and a lollipop
and said, "You're a *very* healthy frog!"
and smiled.
"See, Mom," said Froggy.
"I *told* you I was fine!"

Froggy stuck the gold star on his forehead and the lollipop in his mouth . . .

got dressed—

zip! zoop!
zup! zut!
zut! zut!—

then leapfrogged with his mother—
flop, flop, flop—
all the way to the exit.
"Hey, Mom," said Froggy.
"That was fun! Let's come back to see
Dr. Mugwort real soon!"

"Not *too* soon!" said Dr. Mugwort,
waving good-bye.